DINO-CHRISTMAS

LISA WHEELER
ILLUSTRATIONS BY BARRY GOTT

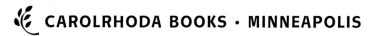 CAROLRHODA BOOKS · MINNEAPOLIS

To all the Dino-Sports fans who have
shared their great ideas with me.
This one's for YOU! —L.W.

For Rose, Finn, and Nandi —B.G.

Carolrhoda Books
A division of Lerner Publishing Group, Inc.
241 First Avenue North
Minneapolis, MN 55401 USA

For reading levels and more information, look up this title at
www.lernerbooks.com.

Designed by Kimberly Morales.
Main body text set in Churchward Samoa 22/36. Typeface provided by Chank.
The illustrations in this book were created in Adobe Illustrator, Photoshop,
and Corel Painter.

Library of Congress Cataloging-in-Publication Data

Names: Wheeler, Lisa, 1963– author. | Gott, Barry, illustrator.
Title: Dino-Christmas / by Lisa Wheeler ; illustrated by Barry Gott.
Description: Minneapolis : Carolrhoda Books, [2018] | Summary: The
    dinosaurs enjoy a variety of Christmas activities, including decorating
    the town, holding a parade, and receiving gifts from Santa Claws.
Identifiers: LCCN 2017040106 (print) | LCCN 2017053240 (ebook) |
    ISBN 9781541523708 (eb pdf) | ISBN 9781512403152 (lb : alk. paper)
Subjects: | CYAC: Stories in rhyme. | Dinosaurs—Fiction. |
    Christmas—Fiction.
Classification: LCC PZ8.3.W5668 (ebook) |
    LCC PZ8.3.W5668 Dgg 2018 (print) | DDC [E]—dc23

LC record available at https://lccn.loc.gov/2017040106

Manufactured in the United States of America
1-39166-21080-2/13/2018

Dino streets are all aglow
as autumn winds turn into snow.

Everyone is full of cheer.
Dino-Christmastime is here!

Fat flakes stitch a quilt of white,
perfect for a snowball fight.

Raptor races. **Stego** chases.
See the smiles on happy faces.

Pachy pummels! **Compy** flings!
T. rex tries snow-angel wings.

On ice like glass, the dinos skate.
Minmi does a figure eight.

The **Ptero twins** hold hockey sticks.

"Look out!" They pull the same old tricks.

"Hey, you two! That isn't nice."

The twins are ousted from the ice.

Triceratops has frozen toes.
Icicles hang from horns and nose.

They head inside to warm limbs up—
steaming cocoa in each cup.

T. rex and **Raptor** feast on s'mores
and cookies shaped like dinosaurs!

It's Christmas in a few more days.
The dinos set out to amaze
by hanging every decoration
for a BIG-time celebration!

Tricera's group adorns the park
with **green** that glimmers in the dark.

T. rex and friends decide, instead,
to paint the town in festive **red**!

Diplo decks the halls with ease—
hangs tinsel on the Christmas trees.

Triceratops is feeling merry—
lights up every topiary.

Iguano sculpts a beast of snow.
Ankylo eats the mistletoe.

Allosaurus makes each wreath.
She gently hangs them with her teeth.

Troodon's at First and Main.
He paints a giant candy cane.

The **Ptero twins** get in the way,
but **Gallimimus** saves the day.

"Find a safer place to stand."
A paintbrush goes in each twin's hand.

On Christmas Eve, the dinos doze.
They dream of gifts with shiny bows
and toys that fill a speedy sled.
Do they hear *clip-clops* overhead?

The sun comes up as if to say,

"Let's celebrate! It's Christmas Day!"

The trees are lit. The eggnog is made . . .

Time for the Dino-Christmas Parade!

Bass drums beat. A trumpet blares.
Dinos march in perfect pairs.

Twirlers of all shapes and size
toss batons into the skies!

Apatosaurus dressed himself.

He looks just like a giant elf!

The candy float is really sweet!
Ankylo's in the driver's seat.

The **Ptero twins** hide in the back,
hurling snowballs.
"Bull's-eye!" *WHACK!*

They hit **T. rex** between the eyes.

A chase begins!

Now who's surprised?

The last float turns into the square.
Who's that guy with snow-white hair?

Dinos cheer. Applause! Applause!
The main attraction—Santa Claws!

The **Ptero twins** are both a mess.
Did Santa see their naughtiness?

Will they get coal instead of toys?
"Ho-Ho-Ho! Come down here, boys."

Santa reaches in his sack.

Pulls out a snowball.

"Bull's-eye!" **WHACK!**

The **Pteros** smile from ear to ear
as Santa hands out sporting gear.

Tricera gets a racing jacket.
T. rex loves his tennis racket.

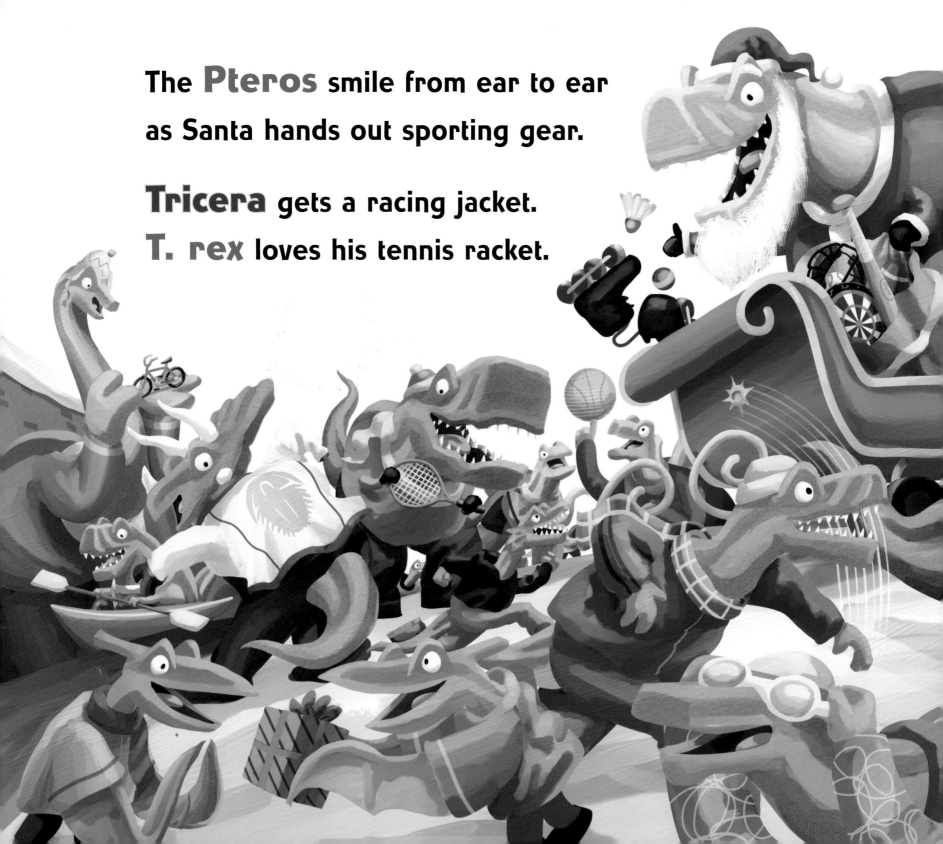

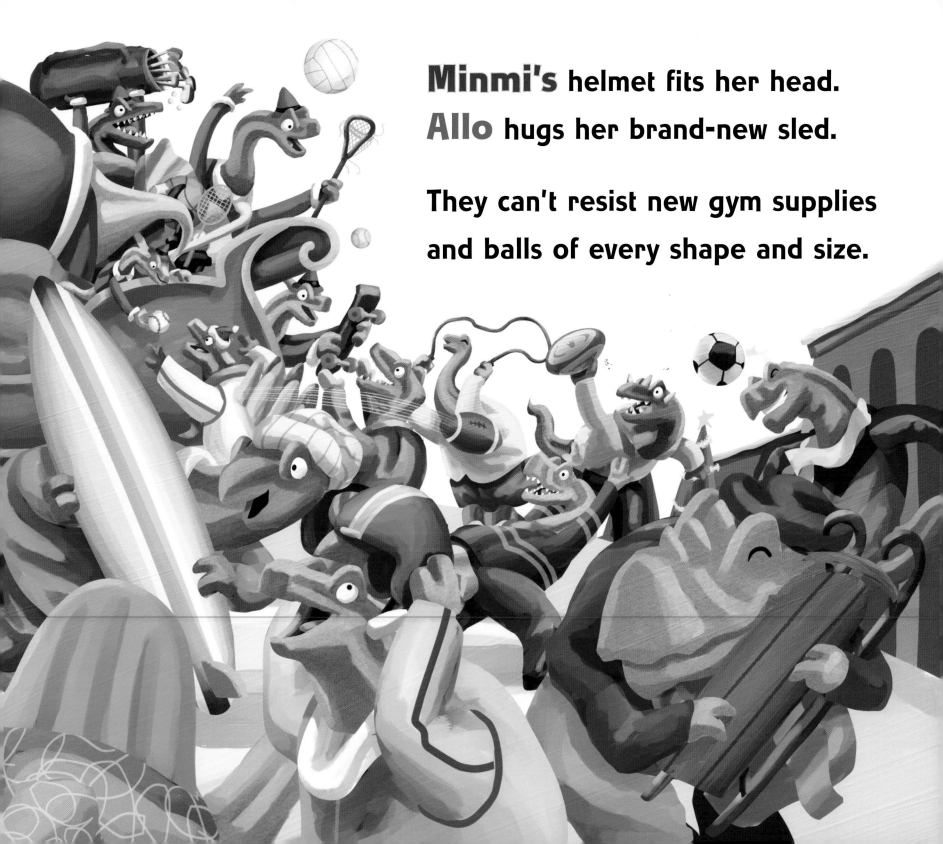

Minmi's helmet fits her head.
Allo hugs her brand-new sled.

They can't resist new gym supplies
and balls of every shape and size.

Afterward, the dinos sing.

The night is filled with caroling.

The soloist is **Stegosaurus**.

Others form a joyful chorus.

Christmas Day is nearly done—
time to plan more holiday fun.

Soon these guys will reconvene . . .

all dressed for Dino-Halloween!